Conestance, Conerad, Cone-Vera and Conen went to sleep very late last night. New Moon was making her way across the sky. Wise Owl was perched on a van, watching what was happening. They found themselves in a most interesting place. Although it was dark, there were lots of things happening. Big lights meant they could watch what was going on.

"Hey! Whatever's going on here?" Conen said.

"I don't understand!" Conerad said.

"I've not seen so many Cones together since we were made in the factory!" Conestance squeaked.

"Those lights are very bright," Cone-Vera said, screwing her eyes up. "I don't get it," Conen said, puzzled. "Cone Collector is putting Cones down, not picking them up. Very strange!"

"Hello, can I help? My name is Conetractor. Come with me. You need Personal Protective Equipment on a building site. Dan, our Project Manager insists on everyone wearing it," she said.

The Cones put on hard hats, eye protectors, gloves and bright jackets.

"Please read the Safety Notice – we must all keep safe on site."

"What is happening here?" Cone-Vera asked.

"This crane is coming to help." Conetractor explained. "It is so big it has to come at night when it is quiet. To keep everyone safe, the humans close the road to other traffic until the crane has passed. The Crane must have a Police Escort. Look, it is so interesting, lots of humans have come out to watch it go by."

"Oh wow! It's our Police Car," Conestance said.

"What's happening to this big bridge? What are the humans doing?" Conestance asked.

"This is one of the main roads into the city," Conetractor explained. "It is called a 'flyover.' It is very old and needs replacing. Thousands of vehicles use it every day so we must keep the road open. Look, all the traffic is driving on the far side while we remove and rebuild this side. Then, we will change sides: traffic on this side while we rebuild the other!"

The Cones watched the big machinery from a safe distance so they wouldn't be seen. Two humans in PPE came by, talking seriously together. They went to speak with Dan.

Conetractor whispered, "It's Kate and Cherie! Come on, let's follow them and see where they are going."

"These two are Structural Engineers," Conetractor explained, pointing.

"What does that mean?" Conen asked.

"'Structure' means a building, a bridge or a stadium. An 'Engineer' on a construction site is someone who understands and is in charge of how things are put together and how they work. Lots of different parts and jobs are needed to make it all work. There's so much to think about and look out for."

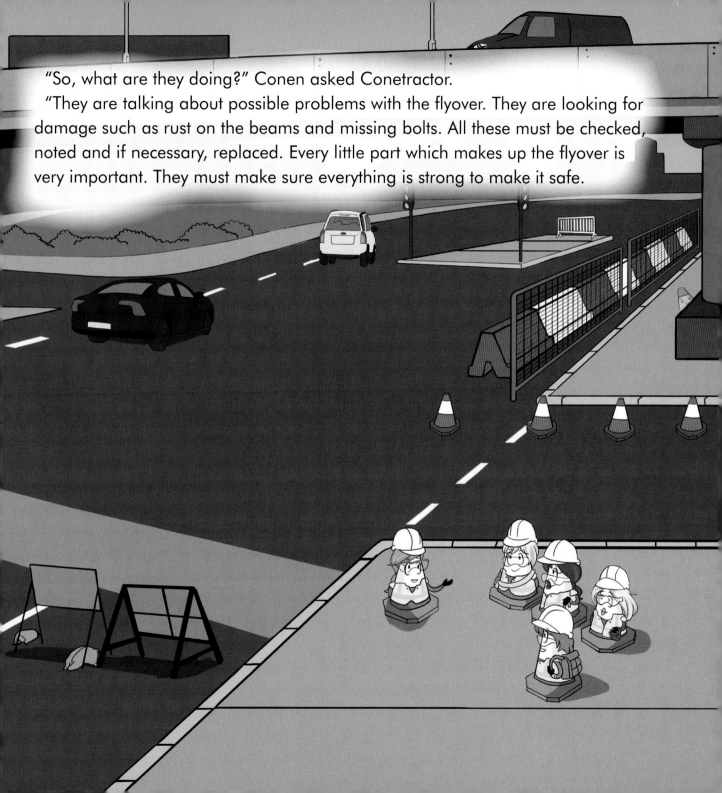

"So, what are they doing?" Conen asked Conetractor.

"They are talking about possible problems with the flyover. They are looking for damage such as rust on the beams and missing bolts. All these must be checked, noted and if necessary, replaced. Every little part which makes up the flyover is very important. They must make sure everything is strong to make it safe.

Conestance noticed someone. "What is that human doing?" she asked, pointing.

"Knocking down and building makes a lot of dust," Conetractor explained. "She is spraying a fine mist of water to stop dust flying about. It helps both workers and people walking by. It is very important work."

Conerad asked what the workers and machinery were doing. "That looks interesting, can we go and see?"

Conetractor took the four friends carefully across the road. They used the Pedestrian Lights to keep safe.

Conetractor pointed. "Look at that tall machine."

"WOW!" Conen said excitedly. "Why does it have a big screw pointing downwards?"

"Come over here and I'll tell you how it works. This is important machinery: it is helping the humans to make the flyover very strong."

"This is called a piling rig. It drives that long metal piece like a huge screw into the ground to make a deep hole. Then, special metal cages are dropped into the holes and concrete is poured in. The concrete sets rock hard making a column called a 'pile.' Together, lots of these make the ground safe to take the weight of this part of the flyover."

"You four are very lucky Cones!" Conetractor said with a smile. "Today you are going to see something really really special. Please don't be frightened as this is one **HUGE** machine! Not many Cones or humans get to see it! We call it SPMT. This stands for Self Propelled Modular Transporter."

"I can't wait," Conen said, his eyes shining with excitement.

"Let's stand here so we get a good view," Conetractor said.

The Cones watched. "The SPMT is extra strong. It can even move aircraft carriers, giant transformers and lots of other extremely heavy objects. It has an engine and lots and lots of wheels. The wheels drive it under the bridge. Then, it picks the bridge up and moves it," Constructor explained.

Conetractor whispered to the four friends, "Now the SPMT has done its job just watch what happens next. The huge crane is removing sections of the road bridge, one at a time."

"Why does the crane need to be so big?" Conerad asked.

"Look how big the sections of the old flyover are! They are very heavy. This is why such a big crane is used. Watch how the crane puts each section onto the back of one of those special trucks. The trucks then take each section to be crushed up, so they can be re-used in other construction projects," Conetractor explained.

"Aaha!" Cone-Vera said. "No waste!"

"Now, I think it's time to show you something else. We need a lift from Cone Collector," Conetractor said. "He will take us to ELOR. I'll explain on the journey."

Fortunately, Conestance, Conerad, Cone-Vera, Conen and Conetractor each ended up on the top of five stacks of Cones. Cone Collector set off. Conetractor said, "I'm taking you to see how a brilliant new road is made."

The Cones became Just Cones, no hands, no faces, no voices, no movements: just cones. Cone Collector drove through a large gate. His driver spoke to Security who opened the red and white striped barrier so they could pass through. Soon they came to a stop in a large yard. "This is ELOR," Conetractor whispered. "East Leeds Orbital Route! Welcome to our brand-new road!"

"Why are the humans making a new road?" Cone-Vera asked.

"There are lots of villages around here. Their roads are narrow; they weren't built for lots of traffic. It is unpleasant for the people who live there with the pollution, noise and danger. We are building this road so that the traffic can get where it needs to go quickly and safely. The villagers can then enjoy cleaner air, peace and quiet and be safer," Conetractor explained.

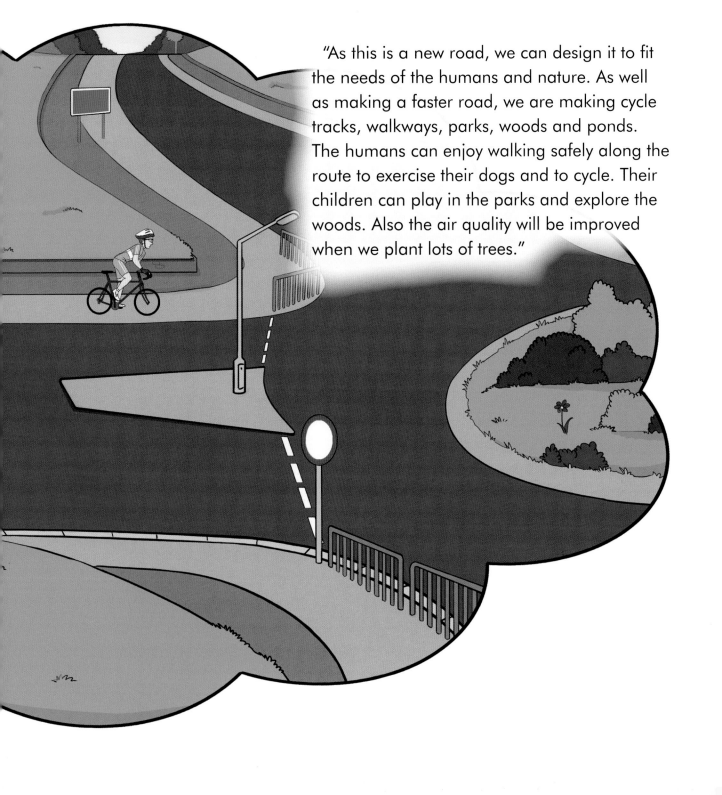

"As this is a new road, we can design it to fit the needs of the humans and nature. As well as making a faster road, we are making cycle tracks, walkways, parks, woods and ponds. The humans can enjoy walking safely along the route to exercise their dogs and to cycle. Their children can play in the parks and explore the woods. Also the air quality will be improved when we plant lots of trees."

"WOW! Look at all those big trucks and diggers!" Conerad exclaimed.

"Yes, they are ready to go to work. A lot of earth needs moving when we make a new road. We must make sure that the route has no sudden hills, dips or tight corners. Vehicles travelling at speed need long straight sections of road with no surprises! All curves and hills need to be as long and gentle as possible," explained Conetractor.

"Did anyone live here before the road building started?" Cone-Vera asked.

"Oh, yes!" Conetractor chuckled. "The use of land changes as time goes by. Humans have lived in different places for thousands of years. Sometimes they had to move around to find food and water. People lived very differently in the days before cars, computers, mobile phones and T.V.!"

"Sometimes their things were forgotten, lost or left behind when they moved away. When we find them, they are like clues about what happened in the past. When we've been working some sites, we have found coins, tools, jewellery and even bits of their homes."

"How very interesting," Cone-Vera said, thoughtfully.

"Here you can see how the big diggers and dumpers have been moving the earth. This part was going to be too steep. They have moved the earth away onto each side of the new roadway. This will make it into a gentle slope as the land rises. Look at how the trucks are bringing and laying out waste stone and concrete which has been broken up into small pieces," Conetractor explained. "Nothing wasted!"

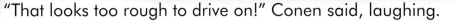

"That looks too rough to drive on!" Conen said, laughing.

"Absolutely!" Conetractor said. "This will be rolled to make a solid base. Then, along comes the Asphalt spreader which will put the smooth, black surface down. The surface is rolled again to make it flat and smooth. Asphalt is very hot, so the workers need to be extra careful. Make sure you don't go near it. Your bases could get stuck in it!"

"Conetractor is saying that you must not think of playing on there!" Cone-Vera said, looking very sternly at Conen.

"The cycle tracks and the walkways are made in a similar way, just using smaller equipment," Conetractor explained.

"How do people get from one side of the road to the other?" Conerad asked. "It's very dangerous to cross a busy road. Will there be crossings with lights?"

"Ooh no!" Conetractor exclaimed. "You can't stop vehicles travelling at 70 miles per hour for people to cross a road!"

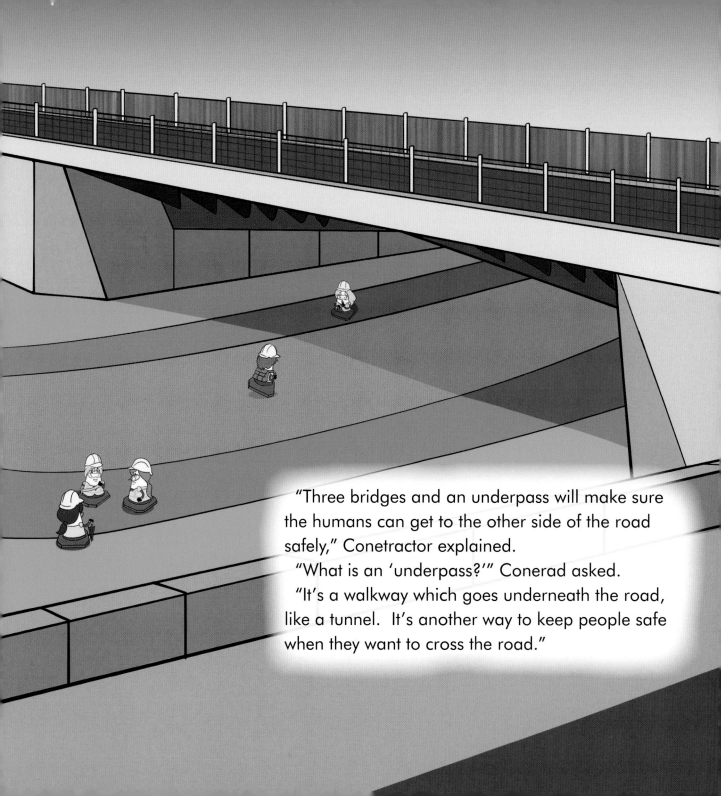

"Three bridges and an underpass will make sure the humans can get to the other side of the road safely," Conetractor explained.

"What is an 'underpass?'" Conerad asked.

"It's a walkway which goes underneath the road, like a tunnel. It's another way to keep people safe when they want to cross the road."

The Cones followed Conetractor through the underpass.

"People will have so much fun with the walkway, the ponds, the cycle track and the park areas," Conetractor said.

"Something is missing on the road," Cone-Vera said.

"There are the steel safety barrier and the signs, there but where are the white lines which keep the drivers safe?"

"If you look, you can see a white-lining truck coming towards us," Conetractor said, pointing.

"I never knew there was so many jobs involved in road-building. Who organises it all?" Conerad asked.

"Let me explain some of the jobs to you," Conetractor said.

"Engineers who make everything work together."

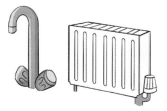

"Plumbers who make sure water is where it is needed."

"Communications staff who let everyone know what to do."

"Electricians who make sure there is power where it should be."

"Quantity Surveyors who make sure there are enough materials to work with."

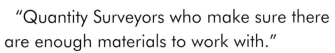

"Machinery, digger and dumper drivers who move things around

"Crane Drivers who lift heavy things into place."

"Payroll staff who make sure everyone gets paid for all their hard work."

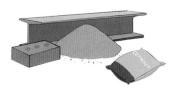

"Thank you, Conetractor, for telling us about road-making and all these amazing jobs," Conerad said.

"Here's a nice quiet spot," Cone-Vera said.

"Sleep-time I think," yawned Conestance.

"Our Cones have had a very busy day. They've learnt a lot abou[t] repairing fly-overs and building roads," Police Car purred.

"Twoohoo, troohooo," Wise Owl hooted softly. She spread her beautiful wings and flew off into the darkness.

New Moon slowly made her way across the night sky, dropping sprinkles of Magic Moondust onto the sleeping Cones.

Good night Cones. See you again soon.